The Magic School Bus®

TO THE RESCUE
>>>>>>>>>>>>>>>>>>>>>>>>>>>>>>>>

FOREST FIRE

Join my class on all of our
Magic School Bus adventures!
Look for these exciting chapter books:

The Truth about Bats
The Search for the Missing Bones
The Wild Whale Watch
Space Explorers
Twister Trouble
The Giant Germ
The Great Shark Escape
The Penguin Puzzle
Dinosaur Detectives
Expedition Down Under
Insect Invaders
Amazing Magnetism
Polar Bear Patrol
Electric Storm

The Magic School Bus®
TO THE RESCUE
FOREST FIRE

SCHOLASTIC INC.
New York   Toronto   London   Auckland   Sydney
Mexico City   New Delhi   Hong Kong   Buenos Aires

Written by Anne Capeci.

Illustrations by John Speirs.

Based on *The Magic School Bus* books
written by Joanna Cole and illustrated by Bruce Degen.

ISBN 0-439-42937-4

12 11 10 9   5/0 6/0

Designed by Peter Koblish

Printed in the U.S.A.   40

First Scholastic printing, September 2002

The author would like to acknowledge
Rose Davis of the National Interagency
Fire Center for her advice in preparing
this manuscript.

INTRODUCTION

My name is Arnold. I am one of the kids in Ms. Frizzle's class.

Maybe you've heard of Ms. Frizzle. (Sometimes we just call her the Friz.) She is a terrific teacher — but a little strange. Science is one of her favorite subjects, and she knows *everything* about it.

She takes us on lots of field trips in the Magic School Bus. Believe me, it's not called *magic* for nothing! We never know what will happen when we get on that bus, and that makes me nervous.

Ms. Frizzle likes to surprise us, but we can usually tell when she is planning a special lesson. We just look at what she's wearing.

I will never forget the day she came to school wearing this outfit. Those forest scenes looked so calm and safe. I thought we might have a normal day in Ms. Frizzle's class for once. Was I ever wrong! Let me tell you all about it. . . .

CHAPTER 1

"Here's an elk!" Wanda said.

"I have some pine trees," Carlos said.

"I've got three deer drinking at a mountain lake," said Phoebe.

No, we didn't have *real* giant trees or wild animals in our classroom. (Unless you count Ms. Frizzle's pet lizard, Liz, of course.) We had pictures of forests and wildlife — lots of them! We were clipping them from nature magazines for our latest science project, a Fantastic Forests display.

"Excellent work, class!" said Ms. Frizzle. She walked from desk to desk with Liz on her shoulder. "All these pictures make me *wild* for wildlands!"

What Are Wildlands?
by Arnold

Wildlands are large areas where plants, trees, and animals live and grow in nature. For the most part, wildland areas are not disturbed by people. That's why we call them wild!

Almost 30 percent of the United States is made up of wildlands in the national parks, national forests, and other special lands.

Sometimes I wish the Friz would be a little *less* wild. But today everything seemed pretty tame. There was no sign of a field trip.

"Here's another picture of a forest," I said, taking a photograph from my shirt pocket. "My uncle Alex sent it to me. It shows the national park where he works."

Hooray for National Parks!
by Tim

    A national park is land that is set aside by the federal government to be kept in its natural state. There are 156 national parks in the United States. The biggest one is Yellowstone National Park, in Wyoming. It covers 2.2 million acres of land.

"Um, Arnold?" Phoebe frowned at the photograph. "That forest doesn't look so fantastic to me. It's on fire!"

"Being around forest fires is my uncle's job," I explained. "He's a firefighter at the Green Hills National Park. See? That's him."

The photograph showed my uncle being lowered from a helicopter in a harness. He wore a hard hat and some protective firefighter gear. Giant flames shot up from the forest behind him. It looked pretty intense.

"Wow. Your uncle must be really brave to fight big fires like that." Tim gave me a funny look. "Are you *sure* you're related?"

Okay, I'll admit it. Just thinking about forest fires makes me sweat. I wouldn't want my uncle's job, but I'm still proud of him.

"What Uncle Alex does is important. And he's the best uncle!" I said. "Last time he came to visit, he brought me fossils and petrified wood for my collection."

"Saving forests from being destroyed by fires is a *hot* job," the Friz agreed. "But forest fires aren't *all* bad. They're a very important part of the wildland ecosystem."

Was I hearing right?

"How could killing trees be good?" I

asked. "Uncle Alex spends all his time fighting forest fires because they're *bad*. Just ask him!"

That was when I noticed a fire that wasn't in the picture of my uncle. It was in the Friz's eyes! I knew exactly what was coming next.

"To the bus, everyone!" said Ms. Frizzle. "I've got a *burning* desire to get the facts on forest fires. A chat with Arnold's uncle is just the ticket!"

I sank down in my chair. Don't get me wrong. I love seeing Uncle Alex. But whenever we go on one of the Friz's field trips, we always get more than we bargained for. Lots more.

"Couldn't we just phone him?" I asked. "The Green Hills National Park isn't anywhere near here."

I should have known a little detail like that wouldn't stop the Friz. She had everyone out the door in a flash.

I was the last one on the Magic School Bus. "Here we go again," I said.

CHAPTER 2

It didn't take long before strange things started to happen. The bus sprouted wings and began to taxi out of the parking lot. In seconds we were in the air.

At least now everyone else would be able to see for themselves how great Uncle Alex is. I looked out the windows of the plane, but then a noise caught my attention.

Beep!

It sounded like an alarm, and it came from a computer screen that was over the dashboard. The screen showed a map of North America with all different swirls of color on it.

"Class, maps like this are used to help

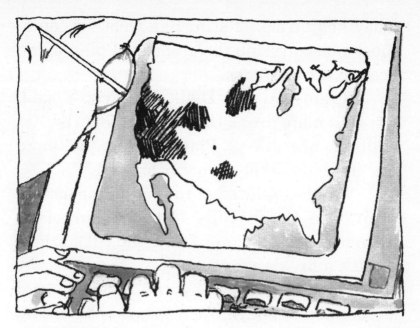

pinpoint areas where wildland fires are most likely to start," the Friz explained.

"I think I read something about that in my book," said Dorothy Ann. (We usually just call her by her nickname, D.A.) She reached into her backpack and pulled out a book called *All About Forest Fires.* Trust me: When it comes to science, D.A. is always prepared.

"It says here that researchers collect information from wildland areas all over the country to make the maps," D.A. told us.

"They keep track of stuff like weather conditions, moisture, and the amount of plants and trees that could burn."

"Right you are, D.A.!" Ms. Frizzle said. "On this map, areas that have a low risk for wildfires are green. Places where wildland fires are most likely to occur are red."

Wanda squinted at the computer screen. "Wait. The Green Hills National Park isn't green at all on this map," she said. "It's bright red. It's a fire danger zone!"

I gulped when I saw the red swirl that surrounded the park. *We're heading right into a danger zone, and it's my fault!* I thought. *If I hadn't shared that photo of Uncle Alex, we wouldn't even be on this field trip.*

After a while, we saw the Green Hills National Park. There was a big parking lot and then tree-covered hills and mountains as far as we could see. Lots of hikers moved along trails that snaked up into the hills.

We were really glad when we spotted a fire truck and a helicopter outside a building near the parking lot.

"Great. That must be the fire station," I said. "The sooner we talk to Uncle Alex, the sooner we can get away from this hot spot! Then we'll all be safe."

But did the Friz stop? No way! She steered the Magic School Plane right past the fire station. Before we knew what was happening, the park buildings were out of sight behind us. All we saw were groups of hikers and trees — a lot of trees.

"We're coming in for a landing!" Ms. Frizzle announced.

She pressed a button, and the Magic School Plane began to shrink and change. Soon it was the size and shape of a pine beetle — with us inside. The Magic School Beetle flitted down onto a pile of leaves on the forest floor.

Everything looked fine, but I still felt pretty nervous. "If this is a hot spot, shouldn't we get *away* from it?" I asked.

"Wildland fires don't just pop up out of thin air," said the Friz. "They need just the right conditions to start."

She opened the glove compartment, pulled out a chart, and held it up.

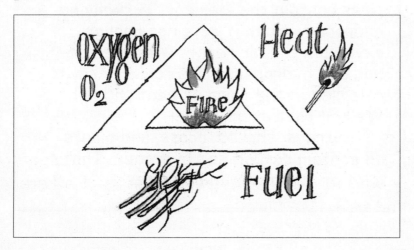

"Let me guess. Fuel is all the stuff in the forest that can burn, right?" said Ralphie.

"You get the picture!" Ms. Frizzle said.

Tim gulped. "Don't look now, but we're *surrounded* by fuel!" he said.

From the Desk of Ms. Frizzle

Fuel for the Fire

All fuels that burn in wildland fires contain the elements carbon and hydrogen. When it gets hot enough, oxygen in the air reacts with the carbon and hydrogen in the fuel. Energy is released in the form of heat and light. We call that energy fire!

Trees, shrubs, grass, and plants all contain carbon and hydrogen. That's a lot of fuel for wildland fires!

The Magic School Beetle was so small that the bushes around us seemed gigantic — like leafy mountains that towered overhead. The trees were even bigger! Each one was like a huge bark-covered skyscraper.

"Fuel can be hot stuff," D.A. said. "But it says in my book that all fuels are not created equal. Water can put out fires. So things that contain lots of water will not burn as fast as drier fuels."

A Word from Phoebe

Flammability is the word we use to describe how easily a fuel burns. The more flammable something is, the more likely it is to catch fire and burn.

"Living plants and trees contain water," Tim pointed out. "Does that mean they're less flammable than dead plants and trees?"

"Absolutely!" said the Friz. "Cool, rainy weather makes fuel in forests less likely to

15

catch fire, too. But hot, dry weather reduces the amount of moisture in fuels and makes them *more* flammable."

Was that supposed to make me feel better? Well, it definitely did not! "My uncle says it hasn't rained here in over a month," I said. "All this fuel must be parched — even the living plants and trees!"

"But a fire still can't start by itself," D.A. pointed out, "not without the other elements of the fire triangle."

"Like oxygen!" Ralphie took a deep breath of air. "It's in the air all around us."

That meant there was just one part of the fire triangle missing — the heat.

How Hot Is Hot Enough?
by Carlos

Fuel has to get very hot before it can catch fire - over 700 degrees Fahrenheit (371 C)! Very dry fuels can ignite at a lower temperature - about 500 degrees F (260 C).

"Uh-oh," said Wanda. She pointed toward a clearing right next to us. Four people sat outside their tent — next to the crackling, red-orange flames of their fire.

Pop!

A fiery spark shot from the campfire and landed on the dry leaves right next to us. A small flame billowed out from the spark.

Oh, no! One tiny flicker is all it takes to make a fire! I thought.

Luckily, one of the campers noticed the flame. He came running over and stomped it out with his sneaker. A second camper poured water from a bucket onto the smoking, charred leaves.

Did you know . . . ?
by Wanda

Human activity is around five times more likely to cause wildfires than lightning is.

"Phew! That was close," I said. "We got lucky." But then we saw something else — towering thunderclouds that darkened the sky over the hills to the west.

A bright, jagged bolt of lightning shot out of the bottom of the cloud. It hit the tree-covered mountainside. My stomach did a flip when we heard the booming crack of thunder that came a split second later.

"Um, Ms. Frizzle?" said Phoebe, biting her lip. "Isn't lightning a source of heat?"

"A sizzling source!" the Friz told us. "A bolt of lightning is three times as hot as the surface of the sun."

This was bad. Way bad. "You mean that lightning could start a wildfire right here in the park?" I said. "Right *now*?"

Lightning Is Hot Stuff
by Carlos

Wildland fires that occur naturally (ones that aren't started by people) are almost always caused by lightning, especially dry lightning. Dry lightning is lightning that strikes when the air is so dry that rain evaporates before it reaches the ground.

A tree struck by lightning can smolder for days before erupting into flames.

Things couldn't get much worse, and it was all my fault that we were in this mess.

As we watched, a plume of smoke rose from the spot where the lightning bolt had struck. It grew thicker, then flames shot into the air.

Ralphie let out a whistle. He said, "Does that answer your question, Arnold?"

CHAPTER 3

In no time at all, the fire began to rise. So did my heart rate!

"Shouldn't we call for help?" I said. "Uncle Alex will want to know about this!"

"Can your uncle and the other firefighters get here in time to make sure all the people get out of the way?" Keesha asked.

"Not to worry," the Friz assured us. "State and national parks have plenty of help on hand to keep people safe during wildland fires."

We were really glad to hear that. Just then we saw some park rangers hike into the campsite next to us. They waited while the campers put out their campfire, packed up their gear, and started down the trail toward the parking lot.

"I'm sure Uncle Alex will be here soon," I said. "But I don't think we should wait. Let's get out of the park before the fire gets any closer."

"Closer?" Ms. Frizzle's eyes twinkled with delight. "Why, Arnold, that's a wonderful idea! We're sure to learn more if we get up close!"

I groaned. Why did I have to open my big mouth?

The Friz hit the gas pedal. The Magic School Beetle spread its wings and flew into the air. We skimmed over the tops of the trees, heading closer to the forest fire every second.

It wasn't long before I smelled smoke. Up ahead, flames leaped off the forest floor, growing bigger every second.

"How did the fire get so big so fast?" Keesha asked. "That lightning just struck a few minutes ago."

"Wildland fires know how to get around,

especially if the conditions are right," Ms. Frizzle explained.

Forest Fires on the Move
by Wanda

The conditions that help wildland fires to start also help them to spread. Dry air, dry plants and trees, and high temperatures make fuels more flammable and more likely to catch fire fast.

Winds help fires to move, too. Winds are like big fans that push fires from place to place. The stronger the wind, the faster the fire spreads. Wind makes it burn hotter, too.

"It's time to face the fire!" the Friz said.

"Shouldn't we *fight* the fire?" Wanda asked.

"Oh, not yet," Ms. Frizzle said. "We have a lot to learn about wildland fires first."

Then she steered the Magic School Beetle straight toward the flames, crying, "Yee-haw!"

The air around us got smokier and broiling hot. The crackling and whooshing sounds of the fire were deafening! Sweat began to pour down our faces.

From D.A.'s Notebook

There are three major kinds of wildland fires:

1 Ground fires spread across grass and low-lying vegetation.
2 Surface fires burn grass, low-lying vegetation, and the trunks of trees.
3 Crown fires are the most damaging and dangerous class of wildland fire. They move across the ground, up the tree trunks, and across the tops of the trees.

"Things never got this red-hot at my old school," Phoebe said.

"Not to worry! I'll put up the heat shield," said the Friz. She pushed a button and a magic see-through shield surrounded the bus. We felt a little cooler then. But we were *not* more comfortable — not with flames spreading. They were like a fiery carpet that gobbled up everything in front of it.

"It looks like this is a ground fire," D.A. said.

Why weren't Uncle Alex and the other firefighters rushing to get here faster?

We saw plenty of creatures that *were* rushing, though. And hopping. And flying. And slithering. Every deer, elk, bird, snake, and squirrel in that forest was trying to get away from the fire!

"I'd feel a lot better if I knew Uncle Alex and the other firefighters were on their way," I said.

That was when the Friz showed us the video link on our computer.

"Whenever we access the link, we can see inside the Green Hills National Park fire station," she explained.

She tapped the keyboard and . . .

"There's Uncle Alex!" I said.

He was sitting at a table in the fire station. So were about a dozen other men and women. Fire-fighting helmets and equipment hung on the wall.

"Why are they hanging around drinking coffee?" I asked. "I don't understand. They don't seem worried about the fire at all!"

"Maybe that's because they know something about forest fires that most people don't," Ms. Frizzle said.

"What's that?" Carlos wanted to know.

"Wildland fires are a part of nature. They *help* forests in many ways," the Friz explained.

I sure didn't see how. When I looked out the bus windows, all I saw were trees and bushes and grass getting burned to a crisp!

Cra-ack!

The sound came from the burning aspen tree right next to us. It was totally surrounded by flames now, and its trunk was charred and black.

"Talk about a towering inferno!" Carlos said. "How can *that* help the forest?"

I wondered about that myself. But Ms. Frizzle didn't have time to answer. An upper branch of the aspen had cracked totally free of the trunk. It was already starting to fall — straight toward us.

CHAPTER 4

I saw a wall of whooshing fire as the burning aspen came crashing our way.

"We're going to be toast!" yelled Tim.

I don't know how Ms. Frizzle did it. In the nick of time, she steered the Magic School Beetle out of the way. We heard a thundering *crash* as the tree slammed to the ground right behind us.

A cloud of hot sparks swirled around us. A split second later, the Magic School Beetle scuttled down into a hole between the roots of another tree.

"Hooray! A rabbit's burrow!" Keesha said.

Let me tell you, it was pretty dark in

there — especially after being in that blinding fire. We didn't see any sign of the rabbit that had dug the burrow. The only thing we could see was the scary orange glow that came from the top of the burrow.

"Wh-what if the fire comes down here after us?" Wanda asked.

"Excellent question!" said Ms. Frizzle.

She pushed a button, and the lights of the Magic School Beetle blinked on. Everywhere we looked there was dirt, dirt, and more dirt.

"I don't see anything that could burn," Ralphie said.

"I get it. Dirt is like a layer of protection," said Tim. "It doesn't burn, so the fire stays above the ground where there are plants and leaves and things that *do* burn."

I was glad we were safe — for now, anyway. But we still had some fire issues we wanted Ms. Frizzle to clear up for us.

"How could getting burned to a crisp be *good* for a forest?" I asked.

"Actually, areas of the forest that look burned up have some parts that are left alive," Ms. Frizzle told us. "That's because trees have ways of protecting themselves from wildland fires."

That sure was news to us. We all watched out the windows while Ms. Frizzle steered the beetle-bus around a curve in the burrow. "See those roots?" she said.

We saw them, all right. They were like gnarled wooden fingers that reached deep into the ground around the rabbit burrow.

"Those are the roots of the aspen tree that just fell down," the Friz told us. "The dirt surrounding the roots will keep them from being burned by the fire."

Roots Help to Rebuild Forests
by Arnold

Some plants – like aspen trees and raspberry and rosebushes – sprout from underground roots after wildland fires. That helps forests to grow back quickly.

D.A. nodded. "It says in my book that some trees have thick bark that protects them from wildland fires, too. The bark helps trees like the ponderosa pine and the giant sequoia survive fires."

"I guess a tree's *bark* can really take the *bite* out of forest fires," said Carlos.

"Carlos!" We all groaned.

"Yeah," Tim agreed. "And just because trees can protect themselves doesn't mean forests fires are *good*."

"Oh, but they are!" said Ms. Frizzle. "Take our friends the conifers. They actually *need* forest fires in order to spread their seeds."

Cones for a Conifer
by Phoebe

Conifers are evergreen trees or shrubs whose seeds are contained in cones that hang from their branches. Sequoia, yew, and all pine trees are conifers.

I didn't have a clue what Ms. Frizzle was talking about. I should have guessed that she would find a way to show us.

She pushed a button on the dashboard, and the Magic School Beetle turned back into a school bus. It got smaller, too. Before long, it was the size of an ant. And we were even smaller!

Ms. Frizzle steered the bus along the burrow until we came to the roots of another tree. Then she drove the bus right *underneath* the bark!

"Class, we're on our way to the upper branches of this lodgepole pine," Ms. Frizzle explained. "That's where pinecones, which contain the tree's seeds, are."

The bark on the tree was very thick. It did a great job of keeping the heat from the forest fire away from us, which means the inside of the tree was safe, too. We moved higher up the trunk without getting burned.

After a while, Ms. Frizzle steered the bus out from under the bark. "We're inside one of the cones at the top of the tree now," she announced. "Let's take a look around shall we?"

The Friz opened the bus door, and we all got out. She kept the lights on so we could see. Walking around inside that pinecone was not easy. The wooden scales of the pinecone were bunched really close together. And the outside was sealed with dark, sticky goo that had a strong pine smell.

"Class," said Ms. Frizzle, "the cones of lodgepole pines, jack pines, and other conifers are sealed with a sticky substance called *resin*. Resin keeps the seeds shut tight inside the cone."

Ralphie pointed to a ball-shaped object that was tucked behind one of the pinecone's wooden scales. It was huge compared to us. It was round, with paperlike wings. "Is this a seed?" he asked.

"Right you are!" the Friz told him. "This pinecone contains about a hundred other seeds just like it. Each one is tucked behind one of the cone's wooden scales and sealed in with the special resin."

"It says in my book that some seeds stay sealed inside their cones for years and years," D.A. added.

"But . . . why do the cones need fires to release their seeds?" Keesha wondered.

"That's a hot topic," the Friz said.

Wildland Fires Help Spread Seeds
by Wanda

Wildland fires create enough heat to melt the resin in seed cones. When the resin melts, the cone opens. That allows the seeds to scatter so new trees can grow.

Crack!

All of a sudden, the scales of the pinecone seemed to move. An intense, *fiery* light flooded over us.

"Yikes! I think the forest fire just melted the resin of *this* cone!" said Phoebe. "The pinecone scales are opening up!"

It was really hard to keep our footing with all those seeds dropping out from beneath our feet. No, scratch that — it was impossible!

"Help!" I cried.

Not that anyone *could* help me. We all fell out of the sides of the cone. Everyone scattered in different directions along with the seeds.

Soon I was all alone . . . falling down, down, down toward the fire.

CHAPTER 5

Falling out of that cone was bad enough. You know what was even worse? There was fire *everywhere*! It blazed in the tops of the trees, on the trunks and branches — and all across the forest floor below me.

This was definitely a crown fire now. And I was falling right into it! I closed my eyes and waited for the flames to swallow me.

Then, amid the crackling roar of the fire, I heard a shout.

"Hang on, Arnold! We're on our way!"

It was the Friz! She was behind the wheel of the Magic School Bus. I was really glad to see that the bus had changed into a

helicopter — and that Liz, Phoebe, and Ralphie were on board, too.

"Yee-haw!" cried the Friz. She steered the bus-copter so that it made a swooshing turn below me, and Liz opened the door.

Plop! I fell through the opening and landed on the bus floor. Let me tell you, I didn't waste any time scrambling to my seat and putting on my seat belt.

"You kids are spread out all over this part of the forest," Ms. Frizzle explained. "Just like the seeds from the lodgepole pinecone we were in. Some of those seeds will grow into trees."

Phoebe, Ralphie, and I were glad to hear that. But we were worried, too.

"We're smaller than ants!" said Ralphie. "How are we going to find the rest of our class?"

"The same way Liz and I found you three," said Ms. Frizzle. She pointed to something that dangled from her neck like a pendant. It looked like a small, flat TV. "This special tracking device beeps whenever the

Magic School Bus comes within sight of any-one in our class."

Phoebe watched as the wind pushed flames from the top of one tree to another. "I sure hope we find everyone else soon — before this crown fire finds them!"

The forest fire had definitely gotten worse since we went down the rabbit hole. The flames were higher than ever, and they were moving fast! We had a hard time keeping ahead of them in the Magic School Helicopter.

Forest Fires Can Go High
by Ralphie

Flames from a large wildland fire can reach up to 300 feet (91 m) in the air. That's as tall as a 25-story building.

"I don't get it. Where's Uncle Alex? Can we check the video link again?" I asked.

The Friz pressed a button on the computer keyboard. Right away, the inside of the fire station popped into view on the screen. Phoebe, Ralphie, and I could hardly believe our eyes.

"They're *still* in the fire station?" Ralphie said.

"This isn't like Uncle Alex," I said. "He would never just stand by and let a forest fire burn like this."

"Unless . . ." Phoebe bit her lip. "What were you saying before, Ms. Frizzle? About fires *helping* forests?"

A huge smile spread across our teacher's face. "Excellent question, Phoebe!" she said. "Wildland fires help out in so many ways that firefighters sometimes decide to let fires play their natural role *without* interfering."

I gaped at the flames that shot all around us. "What?!"

"But," the Friz went on, "fires are allowed to burn *only* if they meet some special requirements."

Ms. Frizzle's Forest Fire Do's and Don'ts

Wildland fire managers (the people in charge of sending firefighters to battle wildland blazes) will *only* allow a wildland fire to burn if:

- The fire starts naturally. (All wildland fires started by people are put out right away.)
- The fire remains in wilderness areas that have been studied and selected as places that need fire.
- The fire does not place people's lives or property in danger.
- Weather conditions and the weather forecast are favorable. (It can't be too dry or windy.)
- There are enough people and equipment to put the fire out if it starts to threaten people or property.

"This fire fits the bill in some ways," Ralphie said. "It was started by lightning, not people. As long as it stays inside the park and doesn't threaten people or their homes, maybe Arnold's uncle and the other firefighters will let it burn."

I still felt kind of confused. "How can they tell whether to let the fire burn if they're not even here?" I asked. "They're just sitting around inside the fire station!"

"Your uncle and the other firefighters are busier than they look," Ms. Frizzle said. "They're using a computer map to track the progress of this wildland fire."

Map It!
by Carlos

Once a forest fire has started, fire managers use computer maps and equipment to track and predict the fire's progress.

Computer maps take into account the wind direction, wind speed, fuel types, and moisture level of the area where the fire is burning. If weather conditions change, or if they are expected to change, computer maps predict how those changes will affect the progress of the fire. That makes it easier for fire managers to decide the best ways to fight forest fires.

"Wow," I said. "If professionals like Uncle Alex let wildland fires burn, fires *must* be good for forests."

"Absolutely! Besides helping trees spread their seeds, wildland fires create greater biodiversity in our forests," said Ms. Frizzle.

What Is Biodiversity?
by Phoebe

Biodiversity is the variety of living things in a particular place or habitat. An area with lots of different plants and animals has greater biodiversity than an area with fewer kinds of living things.

"Wildland fires burn in patches, leaving some areas untouched," Ms. Frizzle went on. "New trees and plants that grow in the burned areas share the forest with older trees that weren't destroyed. Since bushes and trees of different ages and types attract different animals, forests where fires have burned have lots of variety."

"Sounds good to me!" I said.

Beep! Beep! Beep!

The tracking device started to beep like crazy. Then Ralphie said, "I see Keesha and Carlos!"

"Excellent!" Ms. Frizzle hit the gas. "We're on our way!"

CHAPTER 6

The Magic School Helicopter zoomed toward the ground. It was hard to see with all the smoke and flames around us. Finally, I spotted Keesha and Carlos. They were standing on the charred, blackened trunk of a burned tree.

Boy, were they glad to see us! They both scrambled on the Magic School Helicopter as soon as the Friz landed next to them.

"Yuck!" said Keesha, wiping the soot from her face and clothes. "This fire is wrecking the whole forest!"

"Actually," said Ralphie, "Ms. Frizzle was just telling us how getting burned is *good* for forests."

"Huh?" Carlos looked really confused. "But when a forest is burned, people can't eat berries from its bushes or enjoy the green patches of grass under the trees."

"Or use the wood from trees to build things like houses and cabinets," Keesha added.

Ms. Frizzle listened as she hit the controls of the helicopter. We took off into the air. We were still missing D.A., Tim, and Wanda.

"Wildland fires *do* wreck the beauty of our forests and destroy trees that can be used to build things," Ms. Frizzle admitted. "But," she went on, "fires also *help* forests by providing a first-rate recycling program."

Fires Give Forests a Fresh Start
by Tim

Dead trees and leaves and plants in forests are always in the process of decomposing. Fires help out by breaking down dead plants to ash very quickly. The ash is extra rich in all the minerals and nutrients new plants and trees need to grow.

"So, getting charbroiled makes the soil healthier and jump-starts the growth of *new* forests," said Carlos.

"Right," the Friz said. "As long as the fire doesn't get too hot, the soil ends up richer."

I looked out the window at all the

burned trees, bushes, and grass. "No wonder Uncle Alex and the other firefighters are watching this fire instead of putting it out."

"There's more good news about wildland fires, too," Ms. Frizzle told us. "A small fire now can help prevent a larger fire later."

From the Desk of Ms. Frizzle

Less Fuel Equals a Smaller Fire

Forests contain a lot of fuel. Dead leaves and trees can build up on the ground. The more fuel, the worse a fire can be. But if the extra fuel is burned in a fire, there is less fuel on the forest floor for the next fire. This can reduce the damage of a fire.

"I guess this is one case where less is more," said Carlos. "*Less* fuel makes forest fires *more* easy to control."

"Exactly," said the Friz.

Beep! Beep! Beep!

Our tracking device was at it again! We kept a sharp look out the bus windows.

"I see Tim, D.A., and Wanda!" Phoebe shouted.

She pointed to a tall lodgepole pine at the edge of the blaze. It was on fire, and the flames were spreading toward an eagle's nest in the tree's top branches. The eagle had flown the coop, but D.A., Tim, and Wanda were still stuck up there! They sat on the nest while flames leaped toward them.

"Tim, Wanda, and D.A. are high and dry. They could become fuel for the fire!" said Carlos.

"Never fear, class. Our turbo-thrusters will get us there in a flash!" Ms. Frizzle assured us.

She pressed a button and the helicopter shot toward the pine like a rocket. We all cheered as Tim, D.A., and Wanda climbed on board. I was relieved that our class was back together.

"That was close!" Wanda plopped down onto her seat and looked out the window at the tree. "The nest we were in is already on fire."

"Which means some poor eagle doesn't have a home anymore," Tim said.

"That's true," Ms. Frizzle admitted. "But wildland fires *create* living environments that animals like, too."

Wildland Fires Let the Sun Shine In
by Wanda

Wildland fires create open areas in forests. That's something snowshoe hares and lots of other animals are attracted to. Woodpecker populations can grow up to 50 times after fires because they feed on bark beetles and other insects that live in the newly burned trees.

Plants like open areas, too. After a fire, sunlight can shine through to warm the earth. This helps surviving trees and new plants and trees to grow and thrive.

"There's going to be lots of open space after *this* fire," Tim pointed out.

Just then the Magic School Helicopter jolted suddenly to the side. The whole helicopter shook.

"What's happening?" Tim asked.

"There's been a shift in the wind, class," Ms. Frizzle told us. "It's changing directions."

"Uh-oh. Does that mean the fire is changing directions, too?" D.A. asked.

All we had to do was look out the window to answer D.A.'s question. "The fire is moving in a new direction, all right," I said. "Straight toward the edge of the park!"

We got really nervous when we saw the roofs of three houses that stood in the woods just outside the park. They were right in the path of the fire. And there was a lot of brush around the houses to add fuel to the fire!

"If your uncle and the other firefighters don't get here soon," said Wanda, "those houses will go up in smoke!"

CHAPTER 7

Watching the wind push that forest fire closer to the three houses made my stomach twist into a huge knot. We had to do something!

"I'm sure Uncle Alex has been doing his best to track this fire," I said. "Why didn't the weather map warn him about the change in the wind?"

"Sudden changes in weather can take fire managers by surprise," said the Friz. "Even when they're using the best computer maps."

"But now that the wind has changed, Arnold's uncle and the other firefighters will be on the move, right?" Keesha asked.

Out of Control!

by D.A.

In 1988, fire managers in Yellowstone National Park decided to let some small wildland fires burn. Then weather conditions changed, and the fires began to burn too fast and too hot. Nearly 800,000 acres of the park were burned.

"Let's check the video link!" said Ms. Frizzle.

Talk about a big commotion! Uncle Alex and the other firefighters were rushing to get their hard hats and radios. They grabbed all kinds of axes and shovels and put everything in a metal box.

"Phew! They're on their way," I said.

At least, it looked that way. Until a man wearing a greasy coverall came into view on our video link.

"I've got bad news," his voice came

57

Ready, Set, Go Fight Fires!
by Ralphie

Want to know what kinds of equipment wildland firefighters take with them on the job? Here's some of the stuff they use:

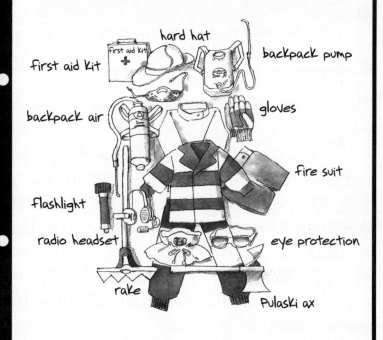

first aid kit

hard hat

backpack pump

backpack air

gloves

fire suit

flashlight

radio headset

eye protection

rake

Pulaski ax

through on our speaker as he spoke to Uncle Alex and the other firefighters. "We've got engine trouble. The helicopter can't take off."

This wasn't just bad news. It was a disaster!

Tim gaped at the fire that burned all around us. "They can't *drive* to the middle of the woods — there are too many trees," he said. "How will they get here to put out the fire?"

"Never fear, class!" the Friz told us. "It's the Magic School Bus to the rescue!"

The next thing we knew, our helicopter-bus grew to the size of a regular helicopter. Except that this helicopter wasn't exactly normal. For one thing, it had a big water tank attached to the bottom of it.

Things changed inside the helicopter, too. We had on special fire-fighting gear. There were metal tool kits filled with Pulaski axes and rakes and shovels. Backpack water pumps and all kinds of other equipment hung from hooks on the walls.

"Why are *we* wearing fire clothes?" I asked.

Ms. Frizzle's only answer was a mysterious smile. "Come on, class," she said. "Let's go get the pros!"

In no time at all, Ms. Frizzle landed the Magic School Helicopter outside the fire station. Uncle Alex and the rest of the firefighters came running out. Did they ever look surprised to see us! But they didn't stop to ask any questions. They climbed right on.

"Uncle Alex!" I said. "It's me, Arnold!"

But you know what? The noise from our

engine was really loud, and my helmet visor and smoke bandanna covered my mouth. Uncle Alex didn't even hear me!

"Let's get this show on the road!" he said.

Ms. Frizzle nodded, and we lifted off.

Reaching Wildland Fires Can Be Hard
by Keesha

Many wildland areas are hard to get to by car or truck. Firefighters have to find other ways to get close enough to fires to fight them. They can go on foot, by parachute, or by helicopter.

Some fire-fighting helicopters called heli-tankers usually come equipped with tanks that can spray water or fire retardant on fires. They can carry firefighters to wildland areas that are hard to get to any other way.

Uncle Alex and the rest of his crew were so busy looking out the windows that they didn't pay much attention to our class. Then we looked out, too, and we understood why.

"Wow. The fire is already closer to the houses," Wanda said.

Wind was pushing the flames up a wooded slope. All that stood between the slope and the houses was a stretch of rocky brush. The fire still had to travel a pretty long way — about the distance of two football fields. But it was getting closer and moving faster every second.

"Look! Other fire-fighting teams are on their way, too," Keesha said.

She pointed at two fire engines that moved toward the houses on a road outside the park. We saw firefighters inside the park, too. Their fire suits made them look like yellow ants as they hiked toward the blaze along the park trails.

"Those engines can't drive onto the field behind the houses," D.A. said, frowning. "There are too many rocks and bushes."

"The firefighters inside the park are still really far away," Carlos added. "They'll never get here in time to stop the fire before it reaches those houses."

"They may not be able to get to the fire in time," said the Friz. "But *we* can!"

She wasn't kidding, either. In just a few minutes, our heli-tanker reached the rocky area between the fire and the three houses.

"There's too much brush for us to land," Uncle Alex said. "We'll have to use the rope and rappel down."

I couldn't believe what happened next. Uncle Alex opened the helicopter door when we were still in the air!

A big gust of wind whooshed all around us. It didn't seem to bother Uncle Alex. He was strapping himself into a safety harness. Then he grabbed the end of a rope ladder that was fastened to the floor by the door. Uncle Alex attached a metal ring to his belt harness and jumped out of the helicopter.

I couldn't even look at that rope without my stomach plunging!

"Come on, class!" Ms. Frizzle jumped to her feet, leaving Liz at the wheel. "Let's take chances! Get smoky! And fight this wildland fire!"

"Us?" My voice cracked. And it wasn't because of the smoke in the air.

The Friz didn't seem to hear me. She was already rappeling down the rope behind my uncle.

"I never dangled over a raging fire at my old school — not even in gym!" said Phoebe.

"Oh, brother," I groaned.

Smoky air whooshed through the open door where the rope hung. I knew Uncle Alex needed help, so I made myself put on a safety harness, crawl over to the helicopter door, and clip a ring onto my harness.

Then I swung my feet over and started to let myself down.

CHAPTER 8

Everything that came next happened in a blur. A big, *fiery* blur.

The fire was still heading toward the houses, and the wind was blowing plenty of heat and smoke our way.

Even from across the rocky field, the roar of the fire was loud. We were all glad for our radio headsets. They made it a lot easier for everyone in our class to communicate.

"What are Uncle Alex and the other fire-fighters doing?" Phoebe's voice came through on the radio once we were all on the ground.

None of the firefighters in Uncle Alex's crew seemed to hear. Their radios were probably on a different frequency. I was just glad that the Friz could hear us. Her voice came through on my radio loud and clear.

"They're forming a line across the field in front of the houses, class," she said. "They're digging a ditch to halt the fire."

"Let's help!" said D.A. "If we all spread out, we can dig a firebreak to keep the fire from getting to the houses."

Firebreaks Put the Brakes on Wildland Fires
by Arnold

A firebreak is a gap across which fire cannot move. A river is a natural firebreak. Firefighters make firebreaks, too. They use saws, rakes, axes, and other tools to remove trees, grass, plants, and anything else that can burn – down to the soil.

The bigger the fire, the wider the firebreak has to be to keep the flames from jumping to the other side.

"I get it. By getting rid of the fuel, we make sure the fire can't spread," said Carlos. "That's a way of fighting wildland fires that I can really dig!"

We all groaned. "Carlos!"

Our rakes and Pulaskis came in really handy. We used them to dig up grass, weeds, and bushes. Uncle Alex and some of the other firefighters had saws, too. They used them to cut down trees that were in the way of our firebreak.

Bigger Isn't Always Better
by Keesha

Big machines like bulldozers and tractor plows can dig up lots of earth fast. Unfortunately, they can also damage wildlands and change the ecosystems of forest areas. If these big machines are used, other crews come in later to restore the land with new plants.

While we worked, I saw Uncle Alex grab a spray nozzle that was attached to the water tank on his back. "Now what's he doing?" I asked.

"According to my book, putting water along the edges of firebreaks makes it even harder for wildland fires to get past," D.A. said. "When the fire engines get here, they'll finish the job."

"I guess it's time to get wet and wild,"

said Ralphie. He pointed at the houses behind us. "Look!"

The fire engines had reached the houses. We could see the heavy streams of water that shot from the firefighters' hoses. Water drenched the houses — and the grass and trees nearby.

"Whoa, look! It's like a giant fire extinguisher," Carlos said.

Fire-fighting Chemicals
by Wanda

Have you ever seen the foam that's sprayed from fire extinguishers? Firefighters use the same kinds of chemicals to cool wildland fires and slow them down. Using the chemicals gives firefighters more time to build firebreaks. Fire-retardant chemicals can be sprayed as a liquid or as a foam.

We looked in time to see a red liquid being sprayed onto the fire from a fire engine. It looked like a giant red cloud.

"Wow," said Phoebe. "With so many people working together, I bet this fire will be under control soon."

Power in Numbers
by Carlos

More than 10,000 firefighters have worked together to fight some bad wildland fires.

"Teamwork is an important part of fighting wildland fires," Ms. Frizzle agreed. "The fire manager at the fire station uses radios to keep in touch with all the crews working to put out this fire."

Phoebe was right! Before long, our firebreak stretched in front of all three houses that were in the fire's path.

I'll admit it. I was proud. We had worked hard to make that firebreak. So hard that something really weird happened. My knees stopped shaking. The big knot in my stomach went away. I guess I was too busy to be afraid!

"The houses are safer now," Wanda said, breathing a sign of relief. "So are the people who live in them."

I was really glad about that. But then I looked through the smoky haze and saw something that *wasn't* safe.

"Hey, guys? There's a fawn! It looks hurt," I said into my radio headset.

A baby deer hobbled out of the woods. It started across the rocky field. While I watched, the fawn stumbled over a rock. It struggled to get up, but it couldn't.

"We have to help!" I yelled.

I ran toward the fawn. With each step, I kept a careful watch on the fire. Very careful. Luckily, the fire was still 50 feet (15 m) away when I reached the fawn.

That was when I realized there was a problem. I was too small to pick up the fawn!

Luckily for me, I wasn't the only one who had come to the rescue.

"Uncle Alex!" I said.

I guess I forgot that his radio was set to a different frequency from mine. He didn't give any sign that he'd heard me. But that didn't matter. We didn't need to talk in order to carry the fawn to safety. Uncle Alex picked up the fawn, and we started back to the others.

At least, we *tried* to.

"Arnold, look out!" Phoebe's scared voice wailed over my radio.

Up, Down, All Around
by Arnold

Whenever you think there is a fire close by, you have to be aware. Always look up, down, and all around so you know the safest way to go.

A burning branch of leaves had blown off a tree that was on fire. It was like a ball of flames that sailed toward us on the wind.

But the worst part was where it landed — right in the tall grass between us and the firebreak where everyone else still worked.

Whoosh!

The dried bushes and grass went up in flames.

"The fire's blocking our way!" I cried. "How do we get back?"

CHAPTER 9

Watching that fire grow, I felt my new courage go up in smoke. Every single one of my fears came rushing back.

"Help!" I said.

I looked behind me, and the fire was coming closer from that direction, too.

"Don't worry, Arnold," the Friz's voice came over the radio. "Help is on the way. Just look up!"

It was the Magic School Heli-tanker! A firefighter was at the controls, but I spotted Liz on the dashboard. The heli-tanker swooped down out of the sky. When it was above the fire that was moving up behind us, a cloud of water sprayed from the heli-tanker's tank.

The flames at the edge of the fire died down and fizzled out.

Phew! That was a big relief. But the brushfire that had sprung up between us and everyone else was still burning — and getting bigger!

Uncle Alex was holding the fawn, so he couldn't do anything about the new fire. It was up to me.

I took a deep breath and grabbed the hose that was attached to the fire extinguisher on my back. I pressed down on the nozzle as hard as I could. A pink spray hit the flames, and the fire was out in a flash. Uncle Alex and I ran to the firebreak with the fawn.

Once we were safe, we turned back to look at the fire.

We all watched while the Magic School Heli-tanker swooped over the fire. It sprayed water on the whole rocky field between our firebreak and the burning woodlands.

"It's coming in for a landing!" said D.A. after the heli-tanker had finished the job. "When we cleared our firebreak, we made enough room for a heli-tanker to land."

I was glad we didn't have to swing in the air on that rope again. We just climbed right on board.

Uncle Alex had given the fawn to one of the wildlife officers who had come to help out. I was glad to know it would be safe.

"Ah." Ms. Frizzle grinned from ear to ear as the Magic School Helicopter lifted off again. "There's nothing like a bird's-eye view to see how a firebreak works."

We hovered overhead and watched out the windows. I was really nervous. I guess I shouldn't have been, though. Thanks to the spray from the heli-tanker, the fire had already died down a lot. When it reached our break, the flames weren't big enough to jump to the other side of the wide path. They got smaller and smaller.

"Without any fuel, that fire doesn't stand a chance," said Tim. "The houses are safe."

"Hooray!" we all cheered.

"Well done, everyone!" We heard Ms. Frizzle congratulate us over our headsets. "Now that this fire is under control, we can go back to the fire station."

That was music to our ears. Everyone was really tired. We didn't say much during the ride back. Until we saw Uncle Alex and the other firefighters point out the helicopter windows, that is.

We saw another patch of charred, burned

forest. The firefighters started talking about a fire they had put out there a year earlier.

"Look closely, class," Ms. Frizzle said. "I think you'll find that this part of the forest has already started to grow back."

At first, all we saw were charred, burned trees and bushes and plants. But then we noticed tender green shoots of new raspberry bushes and aspen trees.

"Those shoots must have sprouted from roots like the ones we saw underground," said Ralphie. "Ones that were insulated from the fire by the dirt around them."

"Yeah," said D.A. She pointed to some bigger, older trees that had survived the fire. "Thick bark insulated those trees so they could survive and make new seeds."

"And a lot of new saplings have taken root, too," Wanda added.

"Excellent observation!" the Friz told her. "Living plants and trees spread their seeds to the burned areas. That helps the forest to grow back faster."

Plants and trees weren't the only living things that were coming back. There were animals, too. Plenty of them! Deer and elk nibbled the branches of the new aspen trees and the raspberry bushes.

"I guess fires can give forests a new lease on life," Carlos said, "if they don't burn too hot."

By the time the Magic School Helicopter landed back at the Green Hills National Park fire station, I was ready to admit that some wildland fires did lots of good things for forests. And it had been really cool working with Uncle Alex to put out the fire.

After we landed, the Friz gave a broad smile. She gave the firefighters a thumbs-up sign as they got off the helicopter.

She waited until Uncle Alex and the other firefighters were inside the fire station. Then she pushed a button on the control panel.

Pop!

In a flash, the helicopter turned back into a bus. We were all wearing our normal clothes again.

"I wish this field trip didn't have to end," I said.

Every single mouth in that bus dropped open. "Are you feeling all right, Arnold?" Wanda asked me.

I was pretty surprised myself.

"Our field trip doesn't have to end yet," Ms. Frizzle said. "Follow me, class!"

We all piled out of the bus and went into the fire station. Let me tell you, Uncle Alex was really surprised to see us. Happy, too.

"It's great to see you, Arnold. I'd love to show your class around. You know, there's a lot more to my job than just putting out fires," Uncle Alex told us as he gave us a tour of the fire station.

"Definitely," I said. "Like watching the weather and tracking fires — and even letting some fires play their natural role."

Uncle Alex sure was impressed by all we knew about forest fires. He started to tell us about the wildland fire that he and the other firefighters had just gotten under control.

Everyone in our class smiled when Uncle Alex talked about the brave firefighters who had come to the rescue and helped fight the fire.

"It's too bad you didn't arrive a few minutes sooner," Uncle Alex said. "You could have met them yourselves."

Hearing that, my grin grew even bigger. "That's okay, Uncle Alex," I told him. "I feel like I know them already."

The Friz's Who's Who
of Wildland Firefighters

Fighting wildland fires is tough work, and the men and women who do it have to be in top physical condition. They have to work long hours in hot, smoky conditions — and carry over 40 pounds (18 kg) of equipment while they're doing it! They also have to know how to use chainsaws, radios, and all kinds of tools safely.

Plus, they take special classes to know how to fight a fire — and how to be aware of what the fire and the weather are doing.

Here are some of the different kinds of wildland fire-fighting crews:

- *Hand crews* fight wildland fires on the ground in places too hard for trucks to get to. Some hand crews, called *hotshot crews*, are specially trained to fight the most dangerous and remote wildland fires.
- *Engine crews* pump water and/or retardant foam from fire engines to fight wildland fires.
- *Air tankers* have airplanes fitted with special tanks for dropping water or fire-retardant chemicals on fires.
- *Heli-tank crews* travel by helicopter to fight fires in areas trucks can't reach.
- *Smoke jumpers* are firefighters who parachute from planes to attack fires in wildland areas that are hard to get to.

After talking with my Uncle Alex, I wanted to pass on some safety tips for people who live near wildland areas.

— Arnold

- Use fire-resistant materials when building or renovating structures.
- Create a safety zone — such as a stone wall, a patio, or a pool — to separate your home from plants that could burn.
- Keep trees trimmed so they don't touch electrical wires.
- Keep trees near buildings free of dead or dying branches and moss. Remove all branches and plant matter from rain gutters.
- Avoid making fires in the open, especially when the weather is hot and dry.